STAR WARS®

THE CLONE WARS™

SLAVES OF THE REPUBLIC
VOLUME FIVE
"A SLAVE NOW, A SLAVE FOREVER"

SCRIPT
HENRY GILROY

PENCILS
SCOTT HEPBURN

INKS
DAN PARSONS

COLORS
MICHAEL E. WIGGAM

LETTERING
MICHAEL HEISLER

COVER ART
BRIAN KALIN O'CONNELL

Jedi slaves! While infiltrating the vicious slaver civilization of Zygerria to find an abducted Togruta colony, Anakin, Ahsoka, and Obi-Wan attend an "auction of a million souls," where the fates of the innocents will be decided.

Unfortunately, before learning the location of the kidnapped people, the Jedi are exposed as agents of the Republic and enemies to the Zygerrian queen, Miraj Scintel. After a fierce battle, the Jedi are subdued and forced into slavery.

To keep his friends alive, Anakin is made to serve as the queen's bodyguard, Ahsoka has been thrown in the dungeon, and Obi-Wan Kenobi and Captain Rex have been transported across the stars to a remote Zygerrian slave-processing facility to begin their own journey into slavery . . .

DARK HORSE COMICS

Spotlight

VISIT US AT
www.abdopublishing.com

Reinforced library bound edition published in 2010 by Spotlight, a division of the ABDO Group, 8000 West 78th Street, Edina, Minnesota 55439. Spotlight produces high-quality reinforced library bound editions for schools and libraries. Published by agreement with Dark Horse Comics, Inc., and Lucasfilm Ltd.

Printed in the United States of America, Melrose Park, Illinois.
092009
012010

♻ PRINTED ON RECYCLED PAPER

Library of Congress Cataloging-in-Publication Data

Gilroy, Henry.
  Slaves of the republic / script by Henry Gilroy ; pencils by Scott Hepburn ; inks by Dan Parsons ; colors by Michael E. Wiggam ; lettering by Michael Heisler.
-- Reinforced library bound ed.
     v. cm. -- (Star wars: the clone wars)
  "Dark Horse Comics."
  Contents: v. 1. The mystery of Kiros -- v. 2. Slave traders of Zygerria -- v. 3. The depths of Zygerria -- v. 4. Auction of a million souls -- v. 5. A slave now, a slave forever -- v. 6. Escape from kadavo.
  ISBN 978-1-59961-710-7 (v. 1) -- ISBN 978-1-59961-711-4 (v. 2) -- ISBN 978-1-59961-712-1 (v. 3) -- ISBN 978-1-59961-713-8 (v. 4) -- ISBN 978-1-59961-714-5 (v. 5) -- ISBN 978-1-59961-715-2 (v. 6)
  1. Graphic novels. [1. Graphic novels.] I. Hepburn, Scott. II. Star Wars, the clone wars (Television program) III. Title.
  PZ7.7.G55Sl 2010
  [Fic]--dc22
                    2009030553

All Spotlight books have reinforced library bindings and are manufactured in the United States of America.

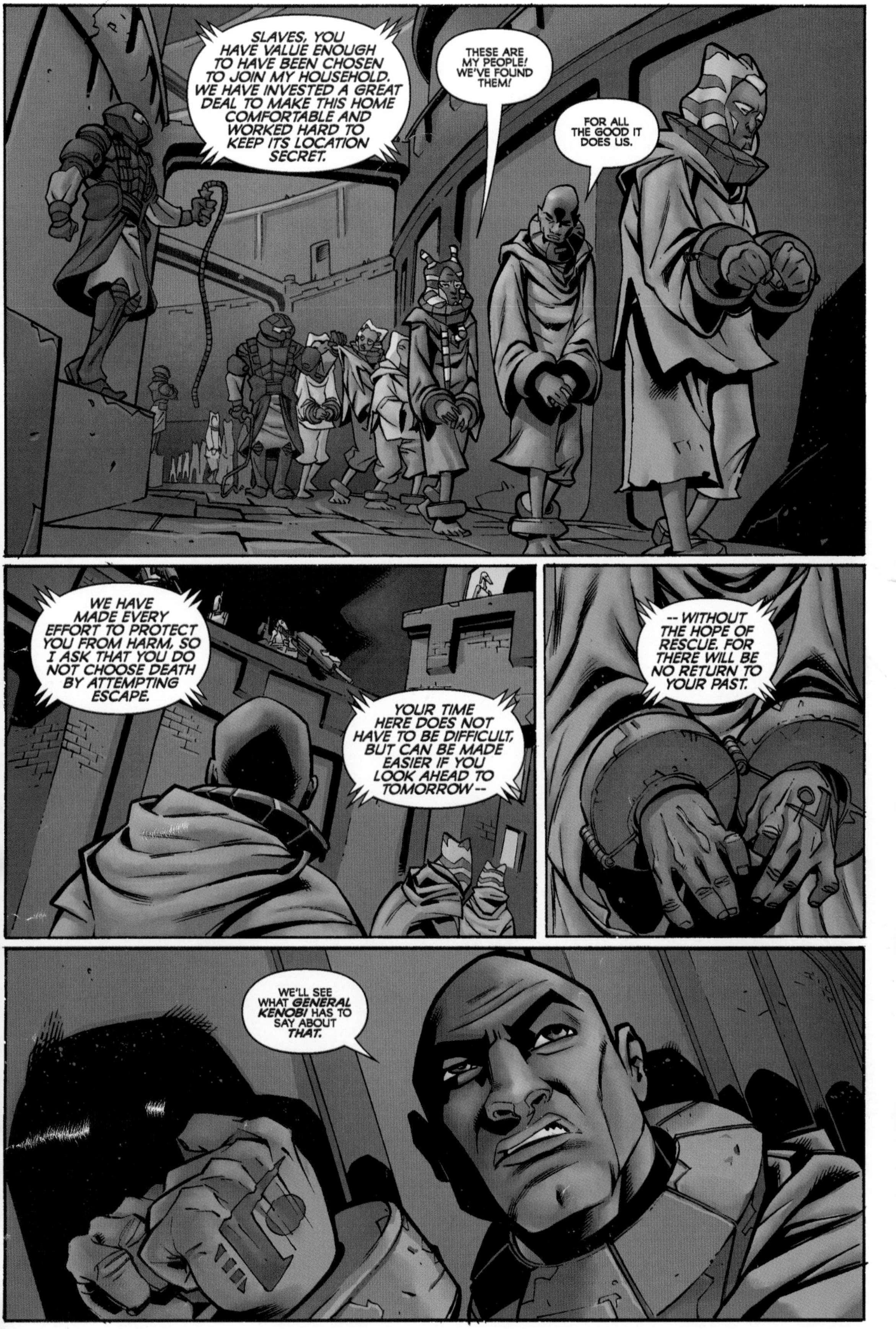
SLAVES, YOU HAVE VALUE ENOUGH TO HAVE BEEN CHOSEN TO JOIN MY HOUSEHOLD. WE HAVE INVESTED A GREAT DEAL TO MAKE THIS HOME COMFORTABLE AND WORKED HARD TO KEEP ITS LOCATION SECRET.
THESE ARE MY PEOPLE! WE'VE FOUND THEM!
FOR ALL THE GOOD IT DOES US.
WE HAVE MADE EVERY EFFORT TO PROTECT YOU FROM HARM, SO I ASK THAT YOU DO NOT CHOOSE DEATH BY ATTEMPTING ESCAPE.
YOUR TIME HERE DOES NOT HAVE TO BE DIFFICULT, BUT CAN BE MADE EASIER IF YOU LOOK AHEAD TO TOMORROW--
-- WITHOUT THE HOPE OF RESCUE. FOR THERE WILL BE NO RETURN TO YOUR PAST.
WE'LL SEE WHAT GENERAL KENOBI HAS TO SAY ABOUT THAT.

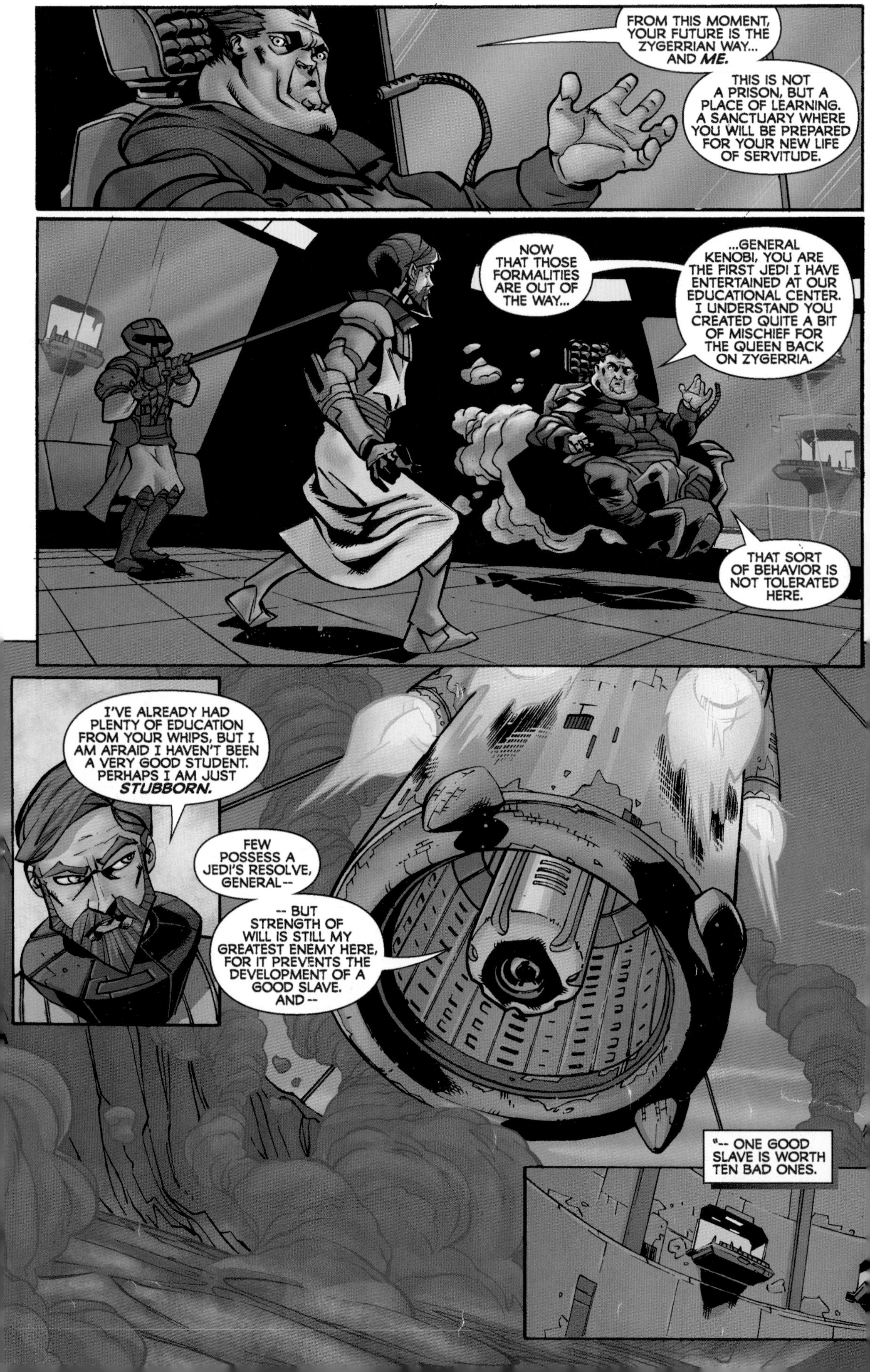
FROM THIS MOMENT, YOUR FUTURE IS THE ZYGERRIAN WAY... AND *ME.*
THIS IS NOT A PRISON, BUT A PLACE OF LEARNING. A SANCTUARY WHERE YOU WILL BE PREPARED FOR YOUR NEW LIFE OF SERVITUDE.
NOW THAT THOSE FORMALITIES ARE OUT OF THE WAY...
...GENERAL KENOBI, YOU ARE THE FIRST JEDI I HAVE ENTERTAINED AT OUR EDUCATIONAL CENTER. I UNDERSTAND YOU CREATED QUITE A BIT OF MISCHIEF FOR THE QUEEN BACK ON ZYGERRIA.
THAT SORT OF BEHAVIOR IS NOT TOLERATED HERE.
I'VE ALREADY HAD PLENTY OF EDUCATION FROM YOUR WHIPS, BUT I AM AFRAID I HAVEN'T BEEN A VERY GOOD STUDENT. PERHAPS I AM JUST *STUBBORN.*
FEW POSSESS A JEDI'S RESOLVE, GENERAL--
-- BUT STRENGTH OF WILL IS STILL MY GREATEST ENEMY HERE, FOR IT PREVENTS THE DEVELOPMENT OF A GOOD SLAVE. AND --
"-- ONE GOOD SLAVE IS WORTH TEN BAD ONES.

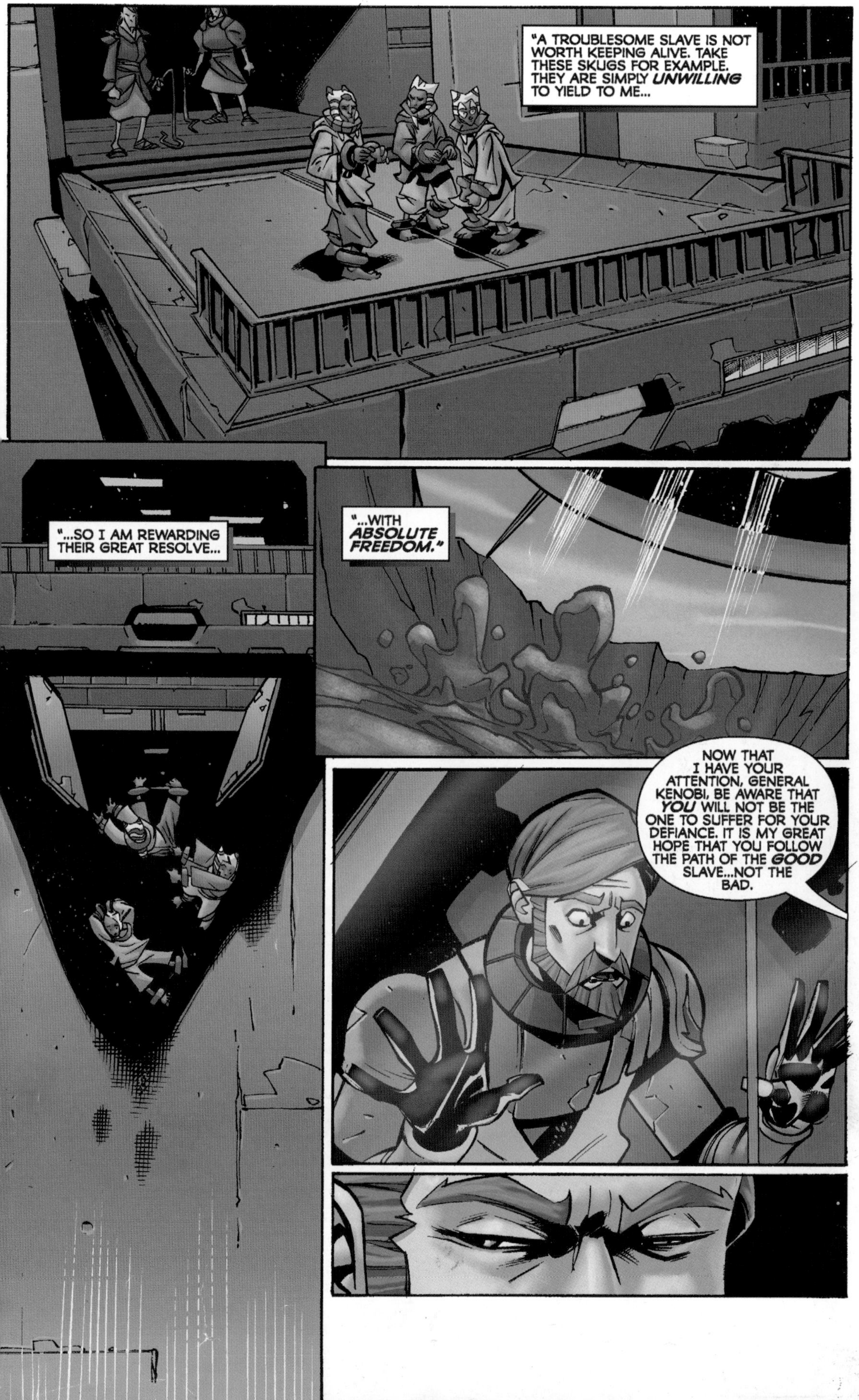
"A TROUBLESOME SLAVE IS NOT WORTH KEEPING ALIVE. TAKE THESE SKUGS FOR EXAMPLE. THEY ARE SIMPLY *UNWILLING* TO YIELD TO ME...
"...SO I AM REWARDING THEIR GREAT RESOLVE...
"...WITH *ABSOLUTE FREEDOM.*"
NOW THAT I HAVE YOUR ATTENTION, GENERAL KENOBI, BE AWARE THAT *YOU* WILL NOT BE THE ONE TO SUFFER FOR YOUR DEFIANCE. IT IS MY GREAT HOPE THAT YOU FOLLOW THE PATH OF THE *GOOD* SLAVE...NOT THE BAD.

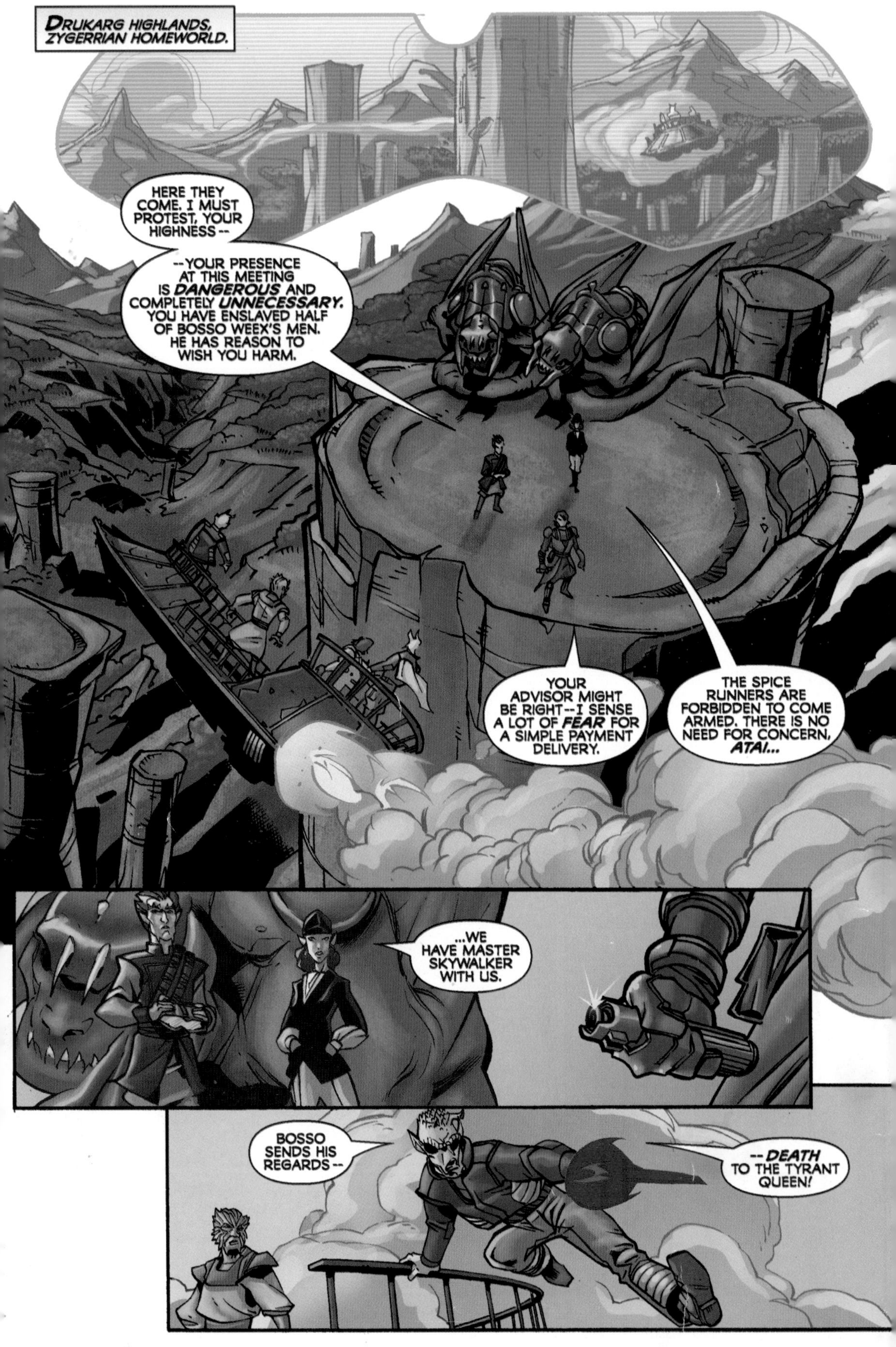
DRUKARG HIGHLANDS, ZYGERRIAN HOMEWORLD.
HERE THEY COME. I MUST PROTEST, YOUR HIGHNESS --
--YOUR PRESENCE AT THIS MEETING IS DANGEROUS AND COMPLETELY UNNECESSARY. YOU HAVE ENSLAVED HALF OF BOSSO WEEX'S MEN. HE HAS REASON TO WISH YOU HARM.
THE SPICE RUNNERS ARE FORBIDDEN TO COME ARMED. THERE IS NO NEED FOR CONCERN, ATAI...
YOUR ADVISOR MIGHT BE RIGHT--I SENSE A LOT OF FEAR FOR A SIMPLE PAYMENT DELIVERY.
...WE HAVE MASTER SKYWALKER WITH US.
BOSSO SENDS HIS REGARDS --
--DEATH TO THE TYRANT QUEEN!

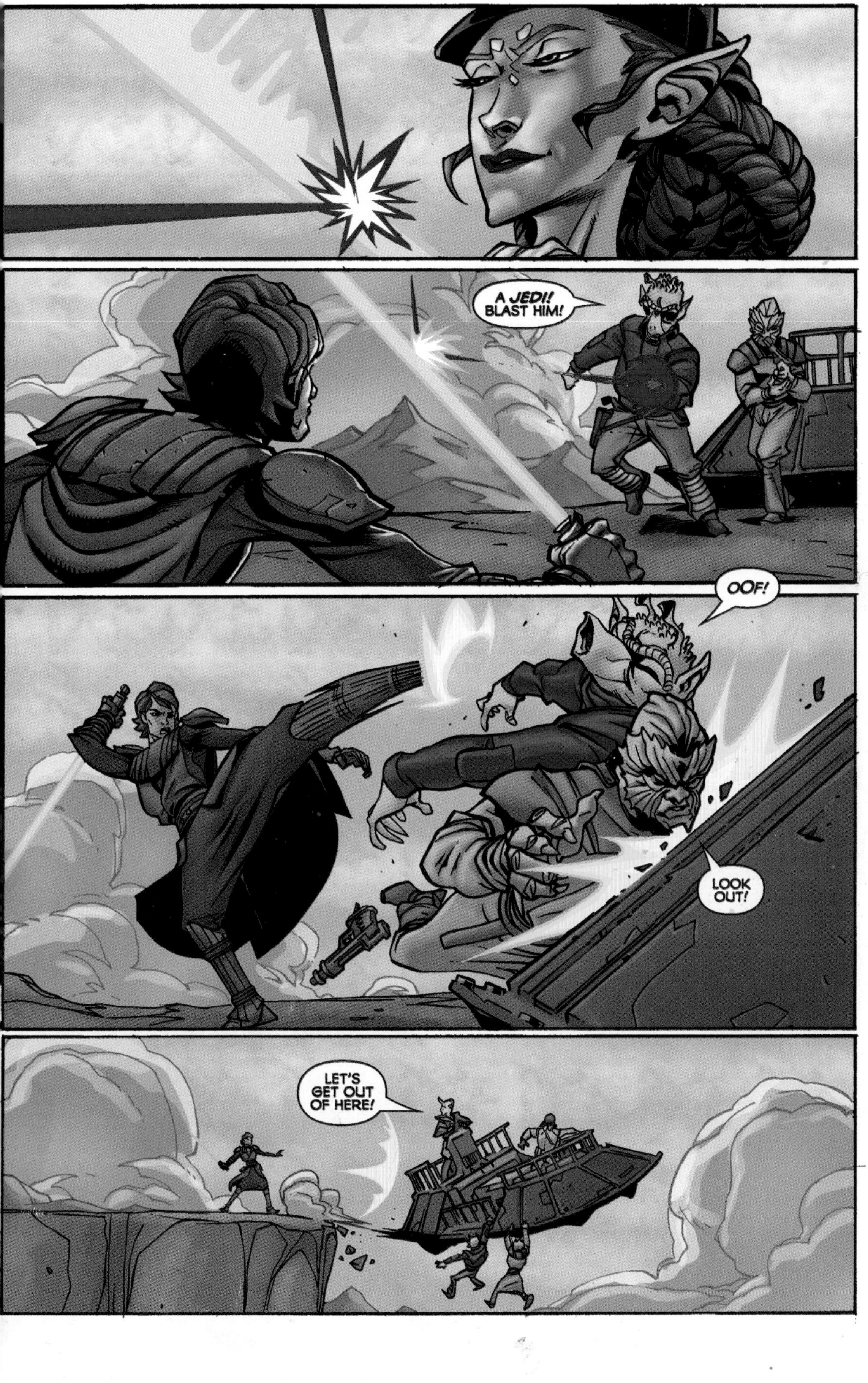
A JEDI!! BLAST HIM!
OOF!
LOOK OUT!
LET'S GET OUT OF HERE!

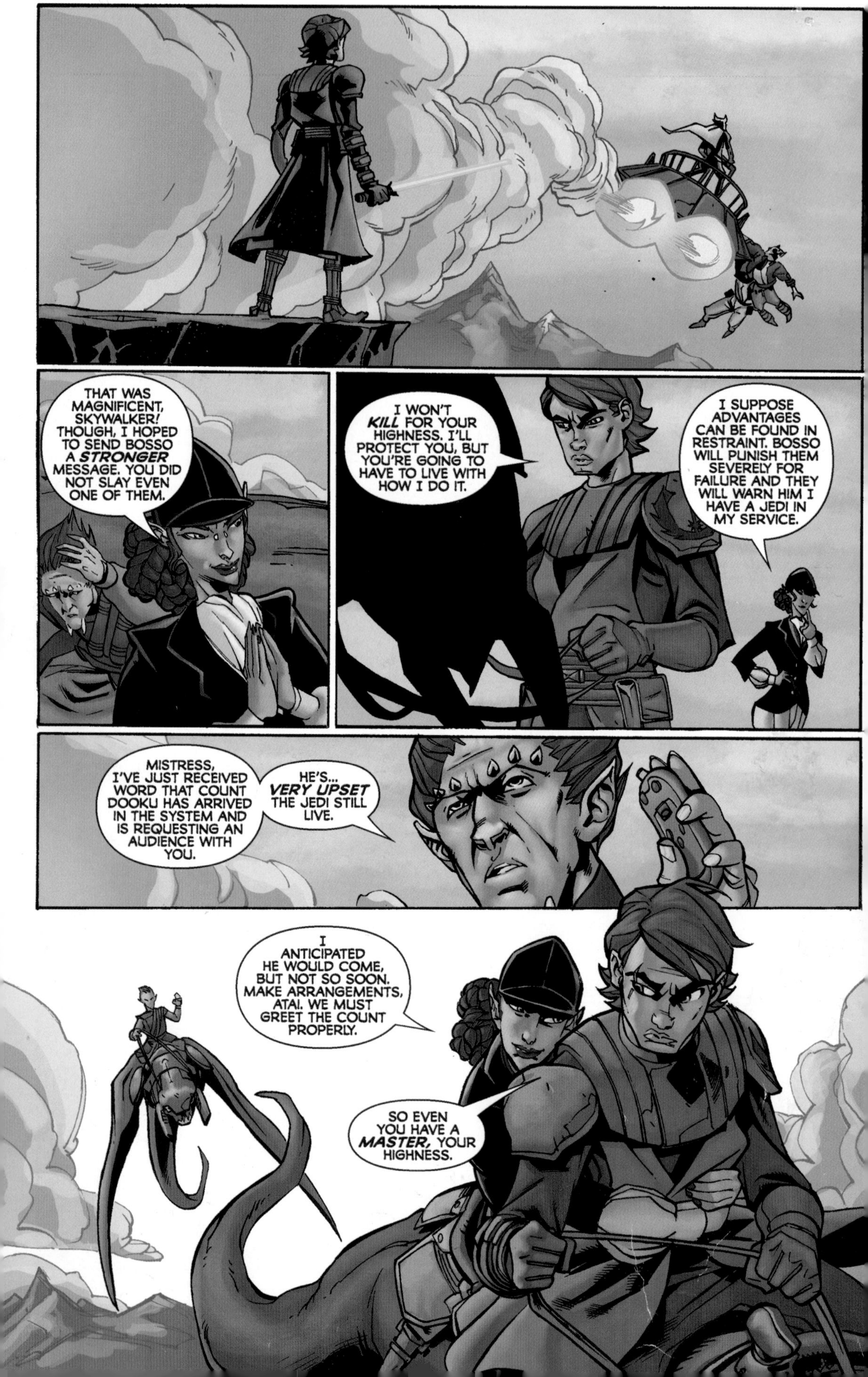
THAT WAS MAGNIFICENT, SKYWALKER! THOUGH, I HOPED TO SEND BOSSO A STRONGER MESSAGE. YOU DID NOT SLAY EVEN ONE OF THEM.
I WON'T KILL FOR YOUR HIGHNESS. I'LL PROTECT YOU, BUT YOU'RE GOING TO HAVE TO LIVE WITH HOW I DO IT.
I SUPPOSE ADVANTAGES CAN BE FOUND IN RESTRAINT. BOSSO WILL PUNISH THEM SEVERELY FOR FAILURE AND THEY WILL WARN HIM I HAVE A JEDI IN MY SERVICE.
MISTRESS, I'VE JUST RECEIVED WORD THAT COUNT DOOKU HAS ARRIVED IN THE SYSTEM AND IS REQUESTING AN AUDIENCE WITH YOU.
HE'S... VERY UPSET THE JEDI STILL LIVE.
I ANTICIPATED HE WOULD COME, BUT NOT SO SOON. MAKE ARRANGEMENTS, ATAI. WE MUST GREET THE COUNT PROPERLY.
SO EVEN YOU HAVE A MASTER, YOUR HIGHNESS.

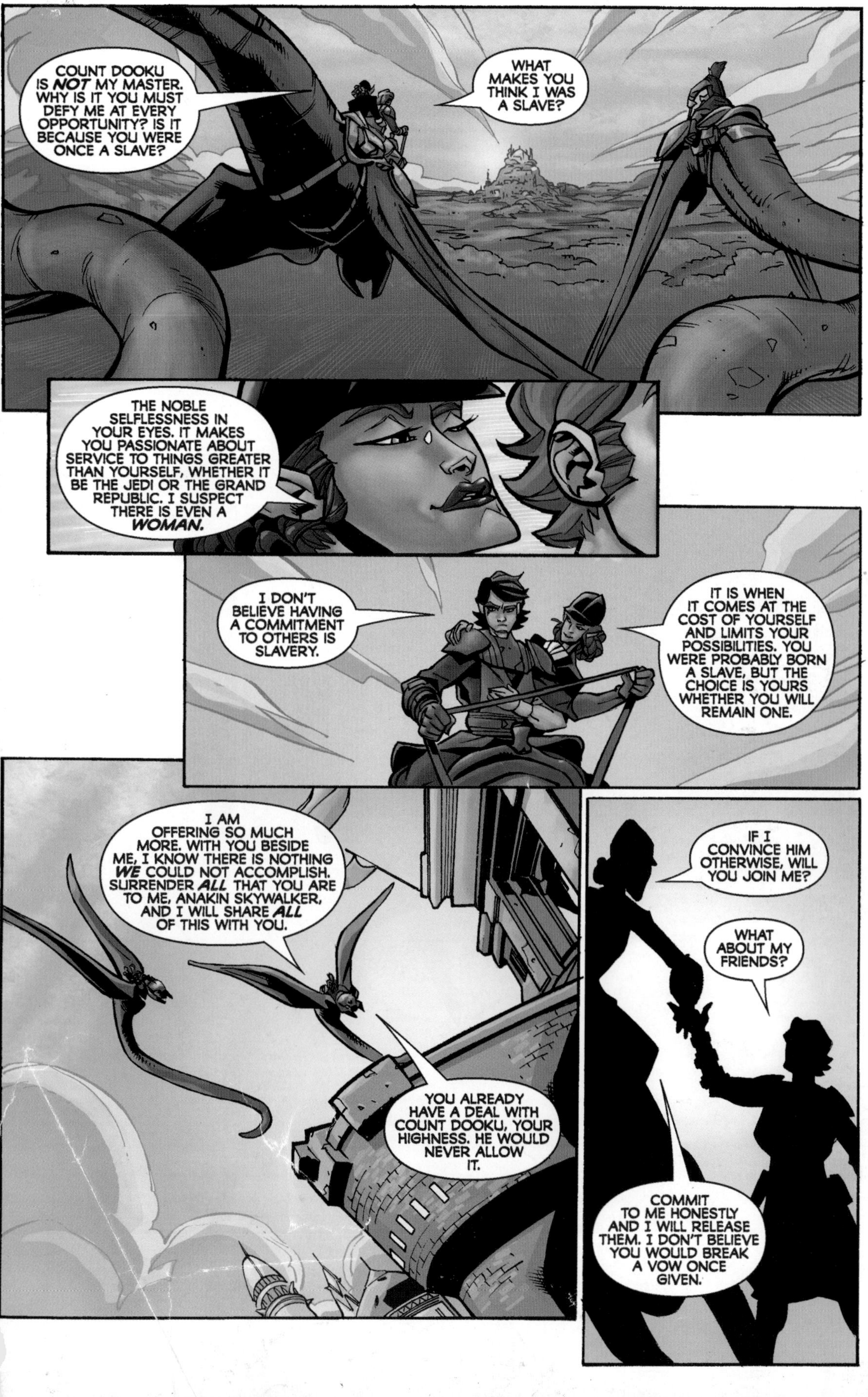
COUNT DOOKU IS NOT MY MASTER. WHY IS IT YOU MUST DEFY ME AT EVERY OPPORTUNITY? IS IT BECAUSE YOU WERE ONCE A SLAVE?
WHAT MAKES YOU THINK I WAS A SLAVE?
THE NOBLE SELFLESSNESS IN YOUR EYES. IT MAKES YOU PASSIONATE ABOUT SERVICE TO THINGS GREATER THAN YOURSELF, WHETHER IT BE THE JEDI OR THE GRAND REPUBLIC. I SUSPECT THERE IS EVEN A WOMAN.
I DON'T BELIEVE HAVING A COMMITMENT TO OTHERS IS SLAVERY.
IT IS WHEN IT COMES AT THE COST OF YOURSELF AND LIMITS YOUR POSSIBILITIES. YOU WERE PROBABLY BORN A SLAVE, BUT THE CHOICE IS YOURS WHETHER YOU WILL REMAIN ONE.
I AM OFFERING SO MUCH MORE. WITH YOU BESIDE ME, I KNOW THERE IS NOTHING WE COULD NOT ACCOMPLISH. SURRENDER ALL THAT YOU ARE TO ME, ANAKIN SKYWALKER, AND I WILL SHARE ALL OF THIS WITH YOU.
YOU ALREADY HAVE A DEAL WITH COUNT DOOKU, YOUR HIGHNESS. HE WOULD NEVER ALLOW IT.
IF I CONVINCE HIM OTHERWISE, WILL YOU JOIN ME?
WHAT ABOUT MY FRIENDS?
COMMIT TO ME HONESTLY AND I WILL RELEASE THEM. I DON'T BELIEVE YOU WOULD BREAK A VOW ONCE GIVEN.

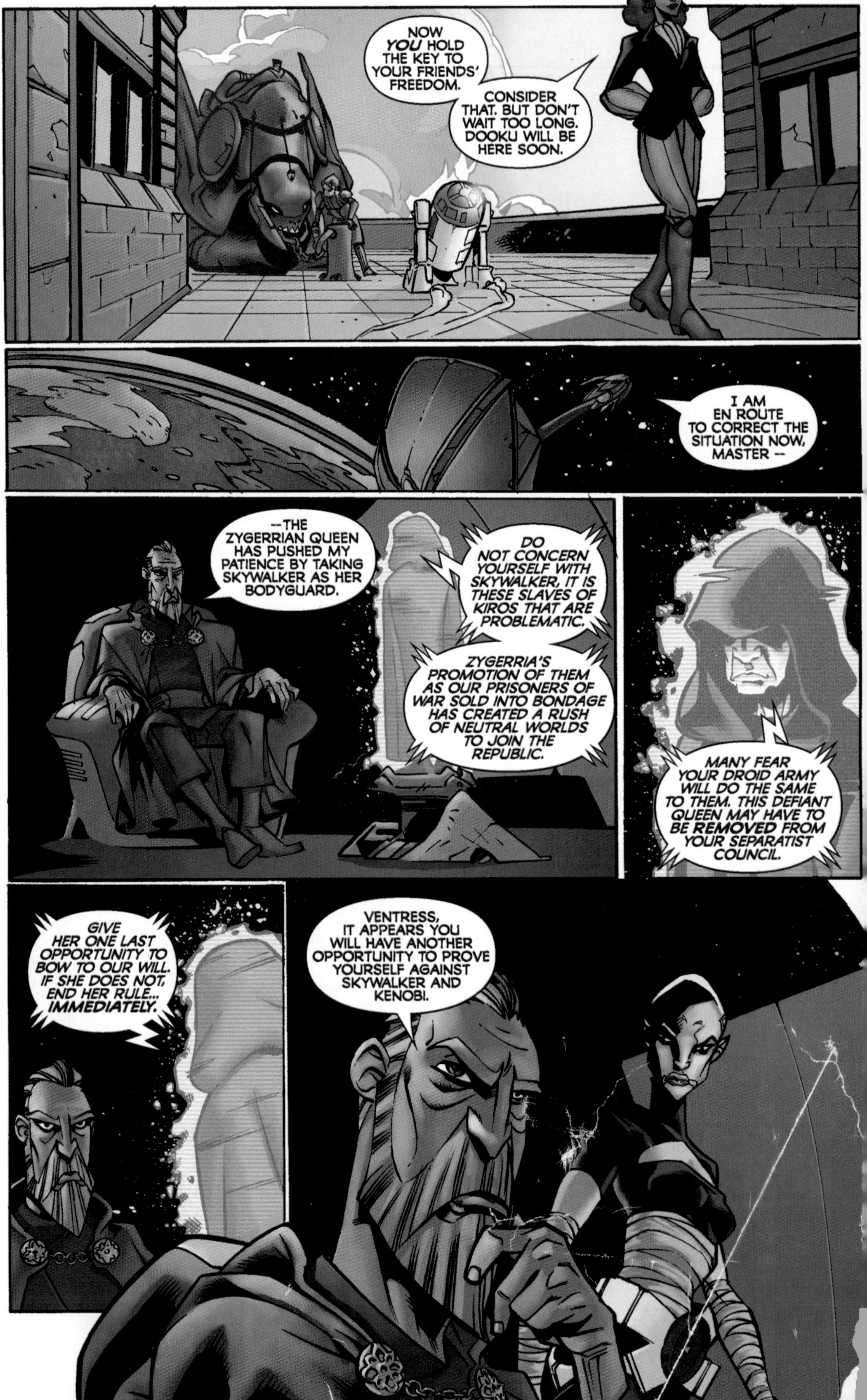
NOW YOU HOLD THE KEY TO YOUR FRIENDS' FREEDOM.
CONSIDER THAT. BUT DON'T WAIT TOO LONG. DOOKU WILL BE HERE SOON.
I AM EN ROUTE TO CORRECT THE SITUATION NOW, MASTER --
--THE ZYGERRIAN QUEEN HAS PUSHED MY PATIENCE BY TAKING SKYWALKER AS HER BODYGUARD.
DO NOT CONCERN YOURSELF WITH SKYWALKER, IT IS THESE SLAVES OF KIROS THAT ARE PROBLEMATIC.
ZYGERRIA'S PROMOTION OF THEM AS OUR PRISONERS OF WAR SOLD INTO BONDAGE HAS CREATED A RUSH OF NEUTRAL WORLDS TO JOIN THE REPUBLIC.
MANY FEAR YOUR DROID ARMY WILL DO THE SAME TO THEM. THIS DEFIANT QUEEN MAY HAVE TO BE REMOVED FROM YOUR SEPARATIST COUNCIL.
GIVE HER ONE LAST OPPORTUNITY TO BOW TO OUR WILL. IF SHE DOES NOT, END HER RULE... IMMEDIATELY.
VENTRESS, IT APPEARS YOU WILL HAVE ANOTHER OPPORTUNITY TO PROVE YOURSELF AGAINST SKYWALKER AND KENOBI.

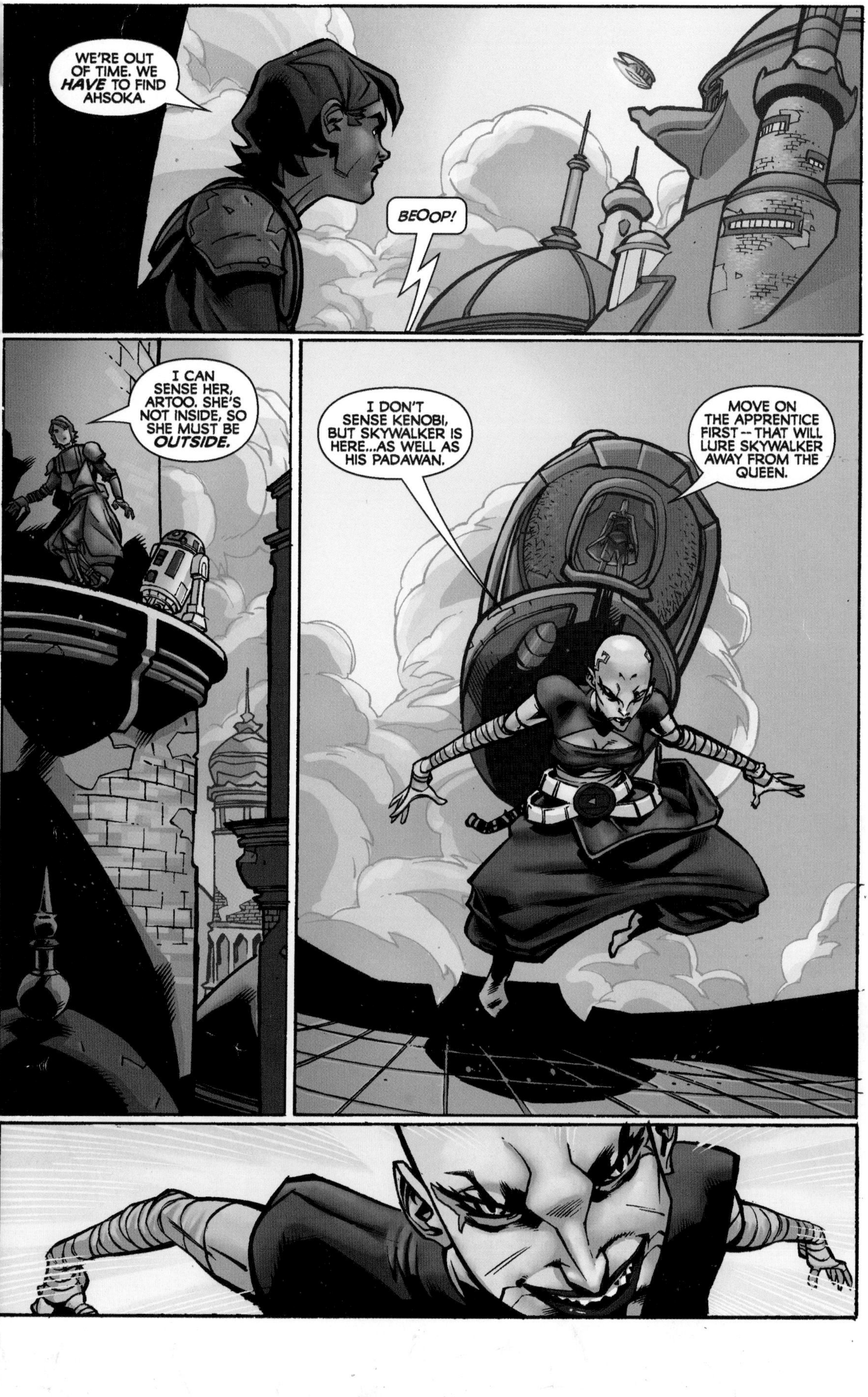
WE'RE OUT OF TIME. WE HAVE TO FIND AHSOKA.
BEOOP!
I CAN SENSE HER, ARTOO. SHE'S NOT INSIDE, SO SHE MUST BE OUTSIDE.
I DON'T SENSE KENOBI, BUT SKYWALKER IS HERE...AS WELL AS HIS PADAWAN.
MOVE ON THE APPRENTICE FIRST -- THAT WILL LURE SKYWALKER AWAY FROM THE QUEEN.

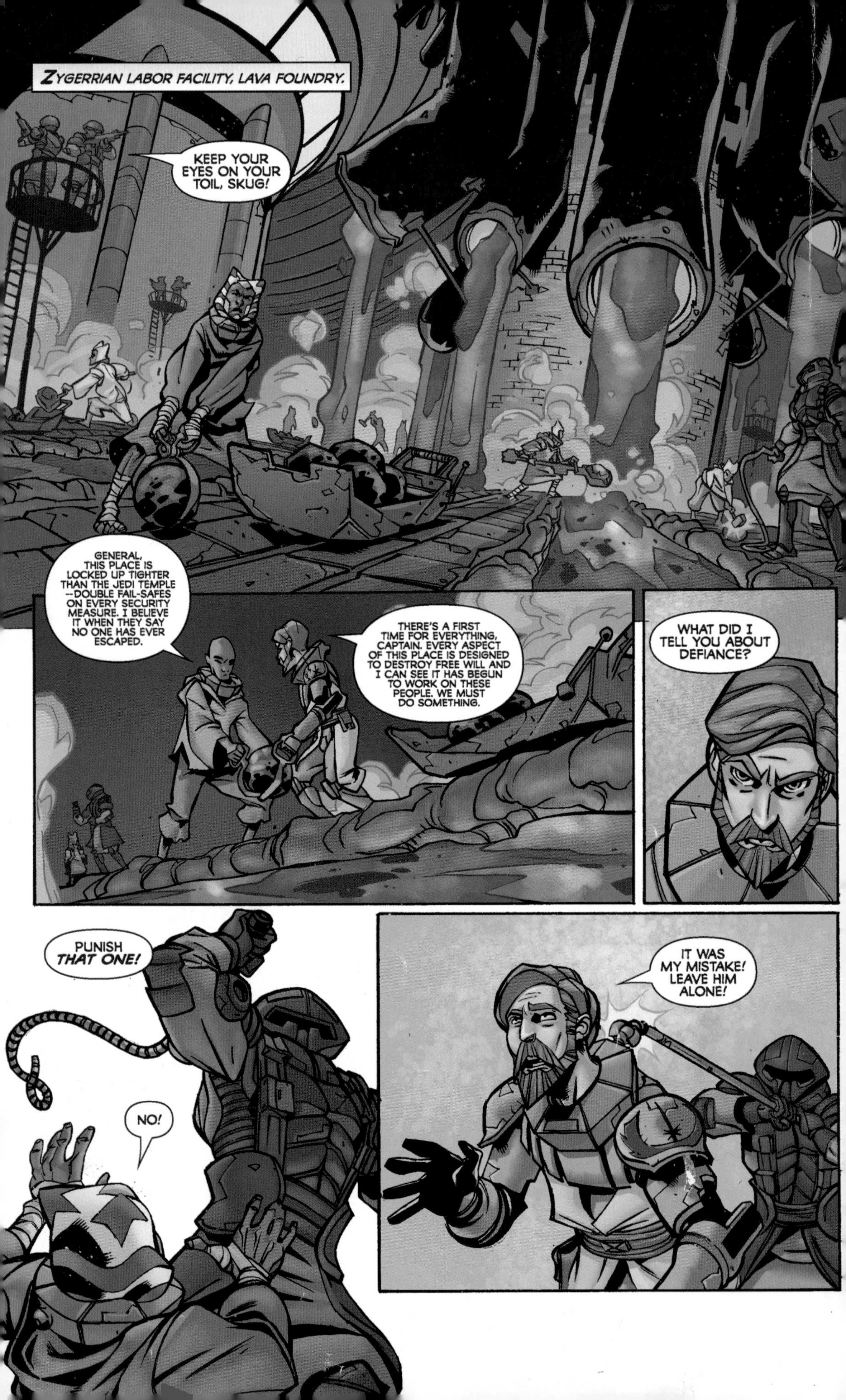
ZYGERRIAN LABOR FACILITY, LAVA FOUNDRY.
KEEP YOUR EYES ON YOUR TOIL, SKUG!
GENERAL, THIS PLACE IS LOCKED UP TIGHTER THAN THE JEDI TEMPLE --DOUBLE FAIL-SAFES ON EVERY SECURITY MEASURE. I BELIEVE IT WHEN THEY SAY NO ONE HAS EVER ESCAPED.
THERE'S A FIRST TIME FOR EVERYTHING, CAPTAIN. EVERY ASPECT OF THIS PLACE IS DESIGNED TO DESTROY FREE WILL AND I CAN SEE IT HAS BEGUN TO WORK ON THESE PEOPLE. WE MUST DO SOMETHING.
WHAT DID I TELL YOU ABOUT DEFIANCE?
PUNISH *THAT ONE!*
NO!
IT WAS MY MISTAKE! LEAVE HIM ALONE!

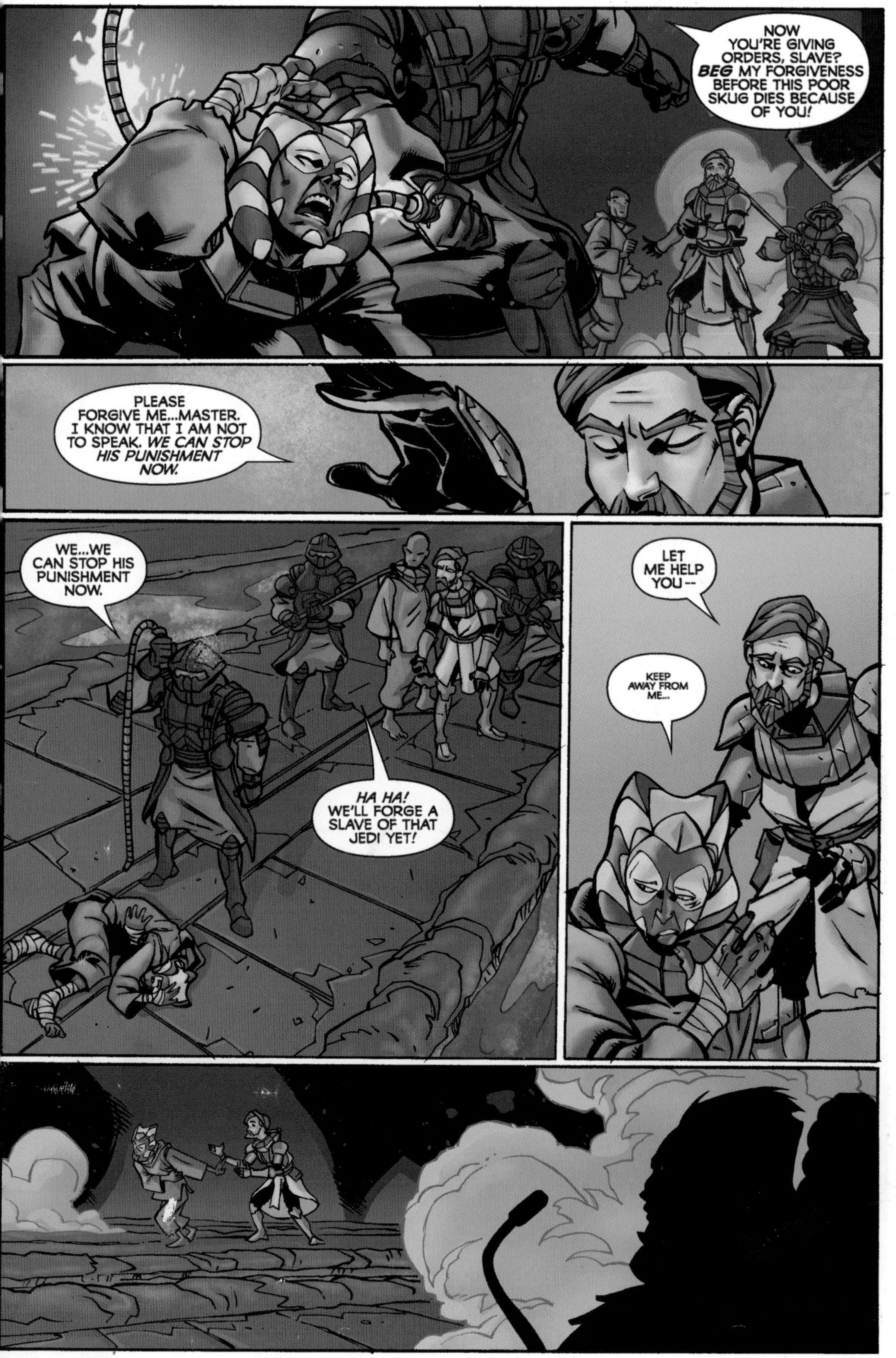
NOW YOU'RE GIVING ORDERS, SLAVE? BEG MY FORGIVENESS BEFORE THIS POOR SKUG DIES BECAUSE OF YOU!
PLEASE FORGIVE ME...MASTER. I KNOW THAT I AM NOT TO SPEAK. WE CAN STOP HIS PUNISHMENT NOW.
WE...WE CAN STOP HIS PUNISHMENT NOW.
HA HA! WE'LL FORGE A SLAVE OF THAT JEDI YET!
LET ME HELP YOU--
KEEP AWAY FROM ME...

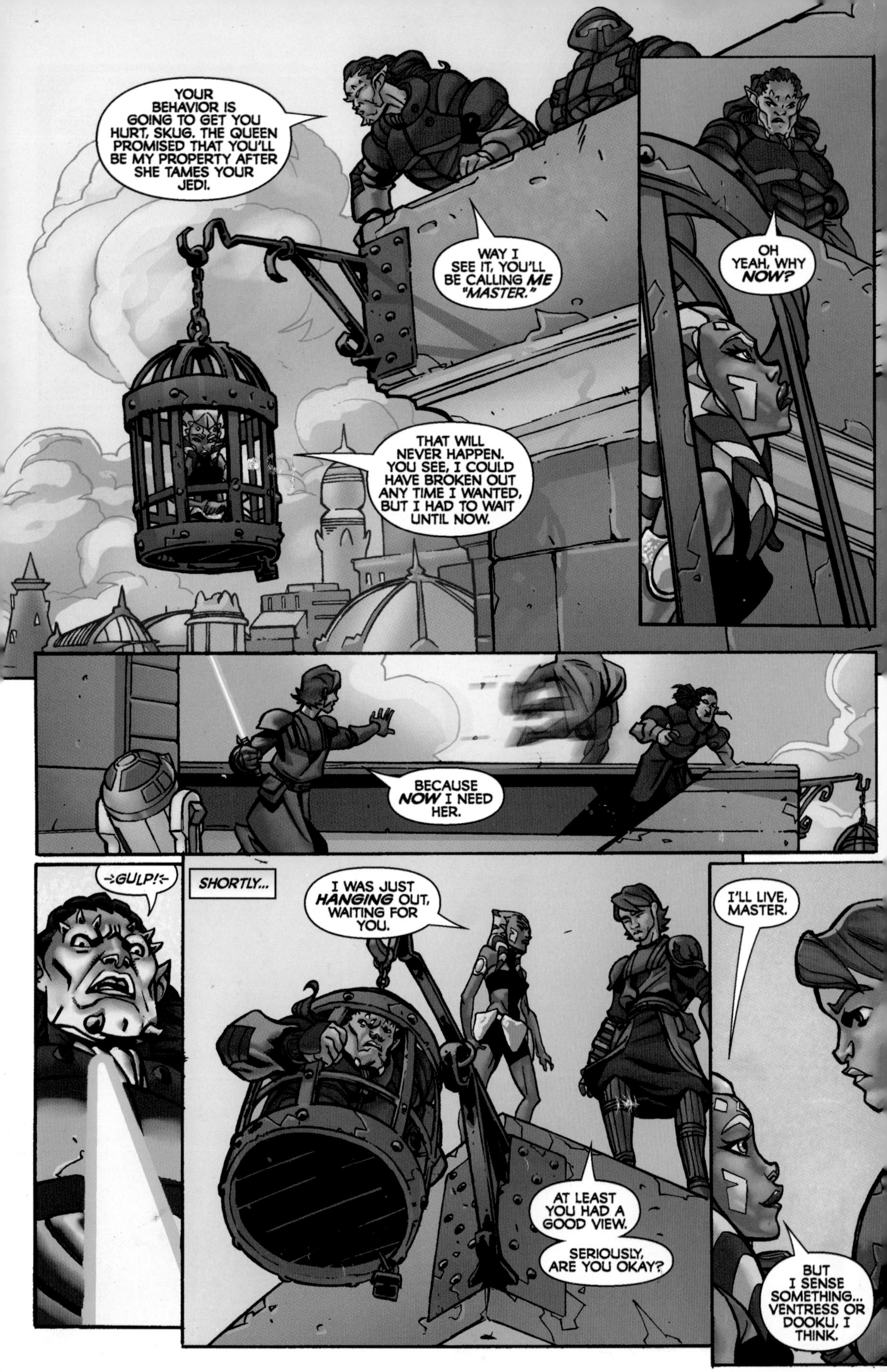

YOUR BEHAVIOR IS GOING TO GET YOU HURT, SKUG. THE QUEEN PROMISED THAT YOU'LL BE MY PROPERTY AFTER SHE TAMES YOUR JEDI.
WAY I SEE IT, YOU'LL BE CALLING ME "MASTER."
OH YEAH, WHY NOW?
THAT WILL NEVER HAPPEN. YOU SEE, I COULD HAVE BROKEN OUT ANY TIME I WANTED, BUT I HAD TO WAIT UNTIL NOW.
BECAUSE NOW I NEED HER.
-GULP!-
SHORTLY...
I WAS JUST HANGING OUT, WAITING FOR YOU.
AT LEAST YOU HAD A GOOD VIEW.
SERIOUSLY, ARE YOU OKAY?
I'LL LIVE, MASTER.
BUT I SENSE SOMETHING... VENTRESS OR DOOKU, I THINK.

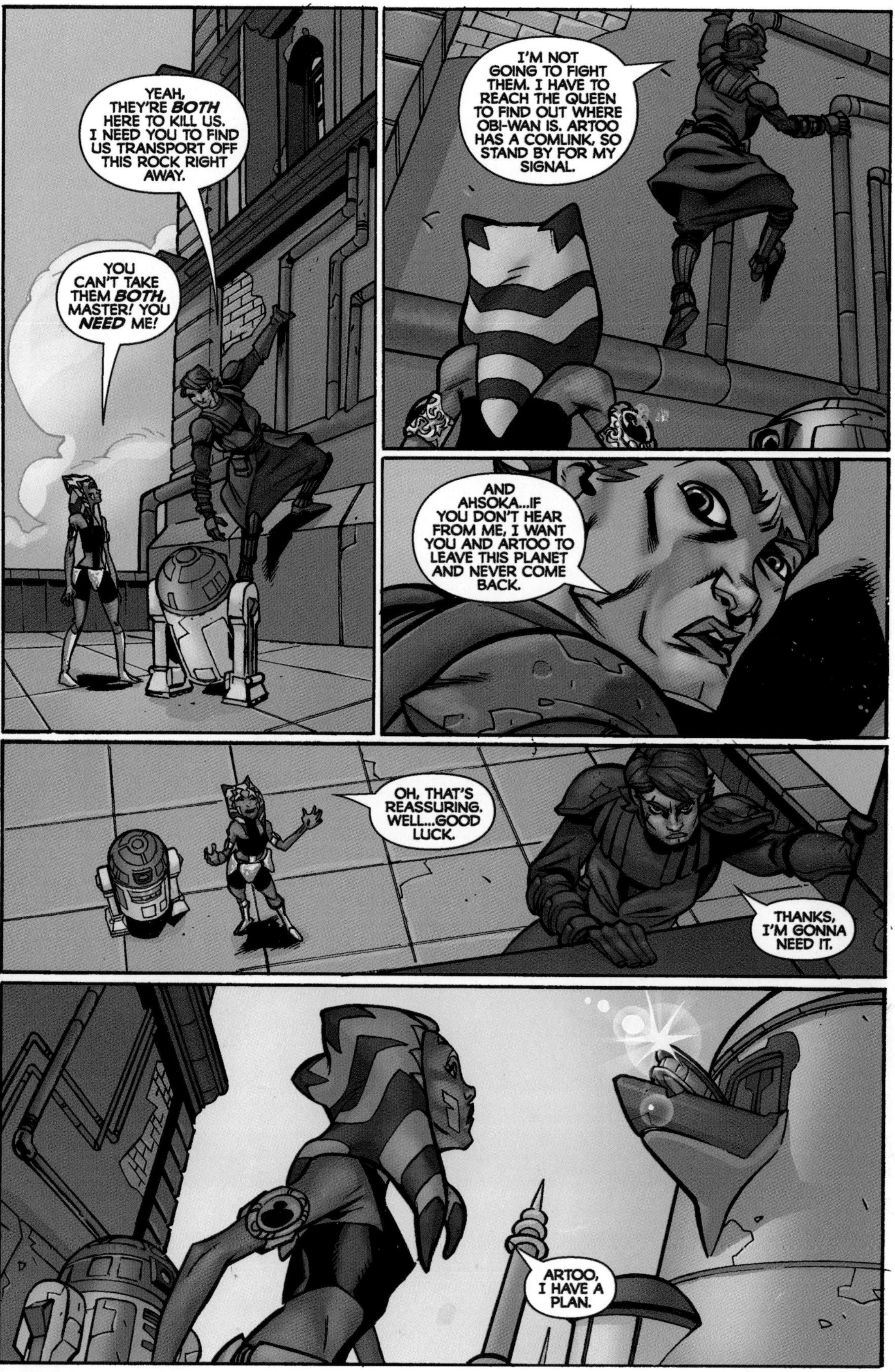
YEAH, THEY'RE *BOTH* HERE TO KILL US. I NEED YOU TO FIND US TRANSPORT OFF THIS ROCK RIGHT AWAY.
YOU CAN'T TAKE THEM *BOTH*, MASTER! YOU *NEED* ME!
I'M NOT GOING TO FIGHT THEM. I HAVE TO REACH THE QUEEN TO FIND OUT WHERE OBI-WAN IS. ARTOO HAS A COMLINK, SO STAND BY FOR MY SIGNAL.
AND AHSOKA...IF YOU DON'T HEAR FROM ME, I WANT YOU AND ARTOO TO LEAVE THIS PLANET AND NEVER COME BACK.
OH, THAT'S REASSURING. WELL...GOOD LUCK.
THANKS, I'M GONNA NEED IT.
ARTOO, I HAVE A PLAN.

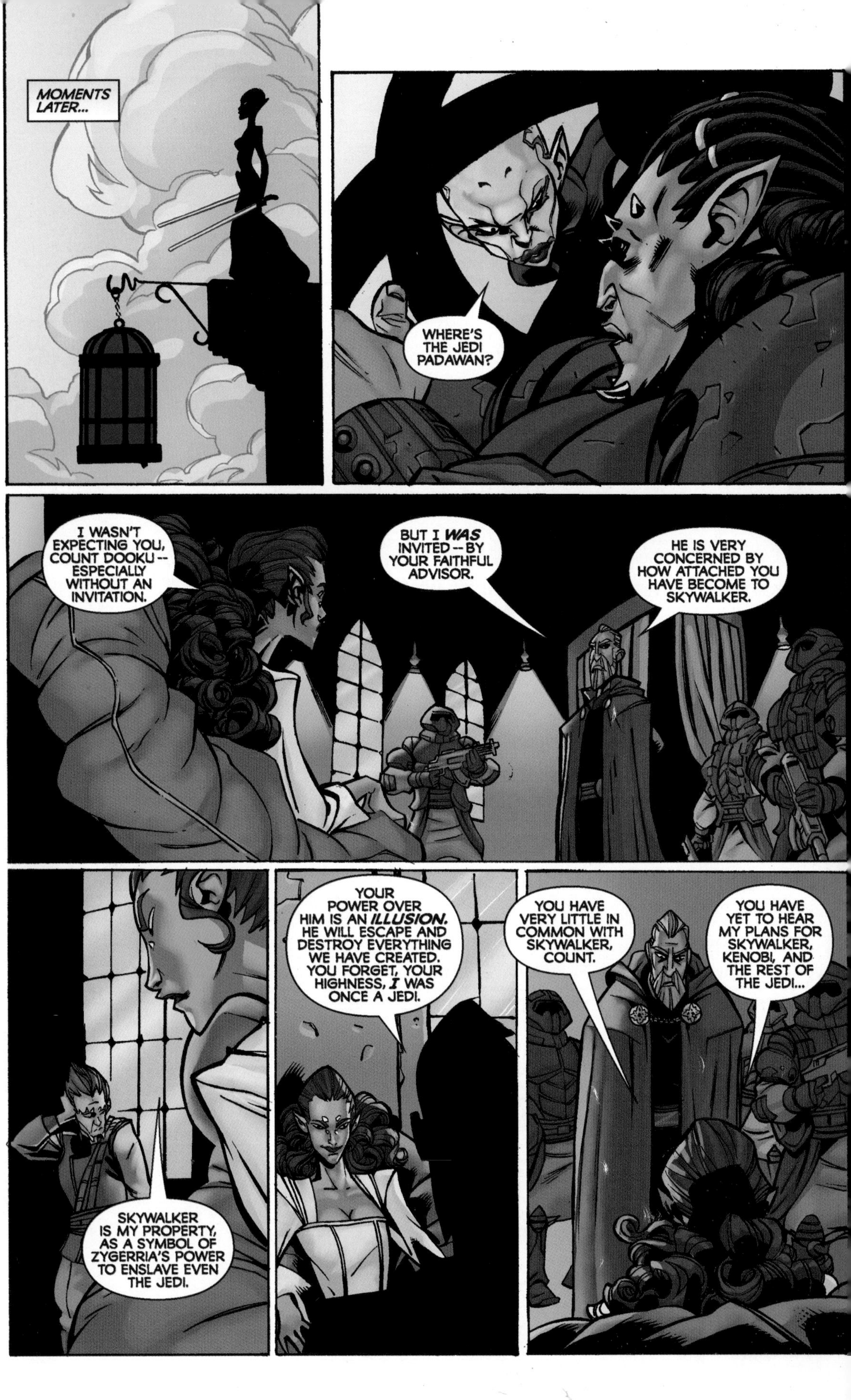
MOMENTS LATER...
WHERE'S THE JEDI PADAWAN?
I WASN'T EXPECTING YOU, COUNT DOOKU -- ESPECIALLY WITHOUT AN INVITATION.
BUT I WAS INVITED -- BY YOUR FAITHFUL ADVISOR.
HE IS VERY CONCERNED BY HOW ATTACHED YOU HAVE BECOME TO SKYWALKER.
SKYWALKER IS MY PROPERTY, AS A SYMBOL OF ZYGERRIA'S POWER TO ENSLAVE EVEN THE JEDI.
YOUR POWER OVER HIM IS AN ILLUSION. HE WILL ESCAPE AND DESTROY EVERYTHING WE HAVE CREATED. YOU FORGET, YOUR HIGHNESS, I WAS ONCE A JEDI.
YOU HAVE VERY LITTLE IN COMMON WITH SKYWALKER, COUNT.
YOU HAVE YET TO HEAR MY PLANS FOR SKYWALKER, KENOBI, AND THE REST OF THE JEDI...

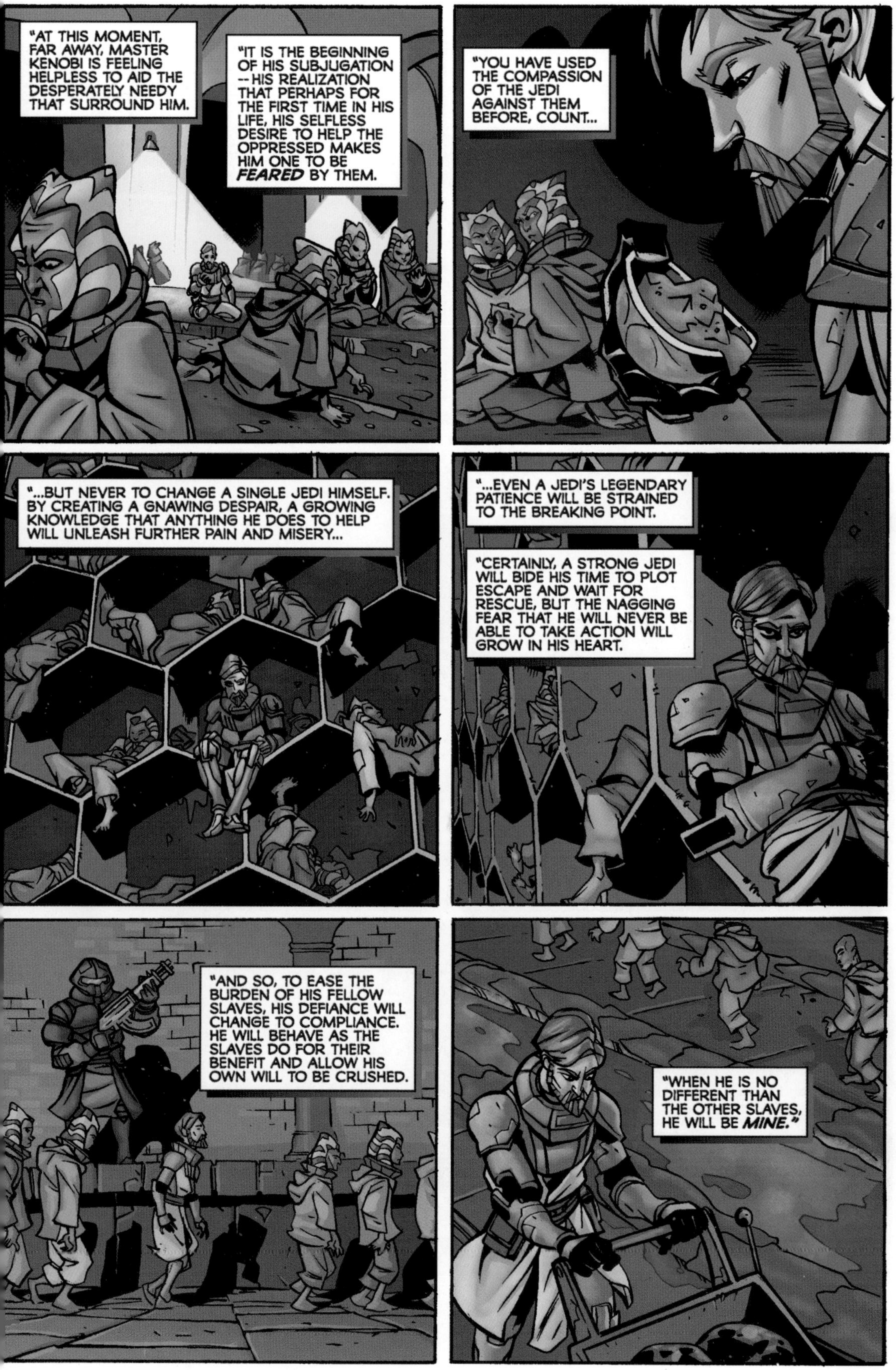
"AT THIS MOMENT, FAR AWAY, MASTER KENOBI IS FEELING HELPLESS TO AID THE DESPERATELY NEEDY THAT SURROUND HIM.
"IT IS THE BEGINNING OF HIS SUBJUGATION --HIS REALIZATION THAT PERHAPS FOR THE FIRST TIME IN HIS LIFE, HIS SELFLESS DESIRE TO HELP THE OPPRESSED MAKES HIM ONE TO BE *FEARED* BY THEM.
"YOU HAVE USED THE COMPASSION OF THE JEDI AGAINST THEM BEFORE, COUNT...
"...BUT NEVER TO CHANGE A SINGLE JEDI HIMSELF. BY CREATING A GNAWING DESPAIR, A GROWING KNOWLEDGE THAT ANYTHING HE DOES TO HELP WILL UNLEASH FURTHER PAIN AND MISERY...
"...EVEN A JEDI'S LEGENDARY PATIENCE WILL BE STRAINED TO THE BREAKING POINT.
"CERTAINLY, A STRONG JEDI WILL BIDE HIS TIME TO PLOT ESCAPE AND WAIT FOR RESCUE, BUT THE NAGGING FEAR THAT HE WILL NEVER BE ABLE TO TAKE ACTION WILL GROW IN HIS HEART.
"AND SO, TO EASE THE BURDEN OF HIS FELLOW SLAVES, HIS DEFIANCE WILL CHANGE TO COMPLIANCE. HE WILL BEHAVE AS THE SLAVES DO FOR THEIR BENEFIT AND ALLOW HIS OWN WILL TO BE CRUSHED.
"WHEN HE IS NO DIFFERENT THAN THE OTHER SLAVES, HE WILL BE *MINE.*"

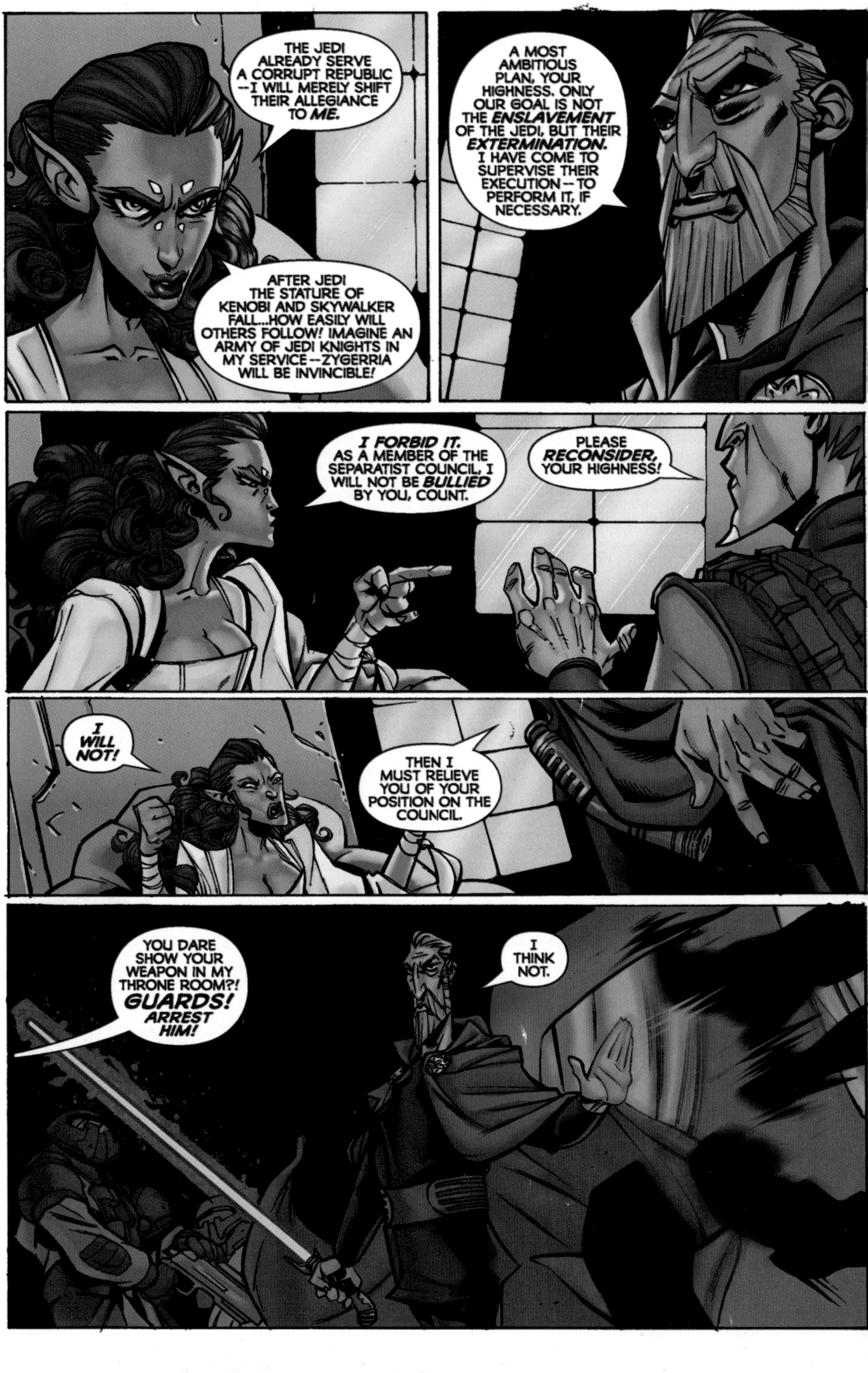
THE JEDI ALREADY SERVE A CORRUPT REPUBLIC --I WILL MERELY SHIFT THEIR ALLEGIANCE TO *ME.*
AFTER JEDI THE STATURE OF KENOBI AND SKYWALKER FALL...HOW EASILY WILL OTHERS FOLLOW! IMAGINE AN ARMY OF JEDI KNIGHTS IN MY SERVICE--ZYGERRIA WILL BE INVINCIBLE!
A MOST AMBITIOUS PLAN, YOUR HIGHNESS. ONLY OUR GOAL IS NOT THE *ENSLAVEMENT* OF THE JEDI, BUT THEIR *EXTERMINATION.* I HAVE COME TO SUPERVISE THEIR EXECUTION--TO PERFORM IT, IF NECESSARY.
I FORBID IT. AS A MEMBER OF THE SEPARATIST COUNCIL, I WILL NOT BE *BULLIED* BY YOU, COUNT.
PLEASE *RECONSIDER,* YOUR HIGHNESS!
I WILL NOT!
THEN I MUST RELIEVE YOU OF YOUR POSITION ON THE COUNCIL.
YOU DARE SHOW YOUR WEAPON IN MY THRONE ROOM?! *GUARDS! ARREST HIM!*
I THINK NOT.

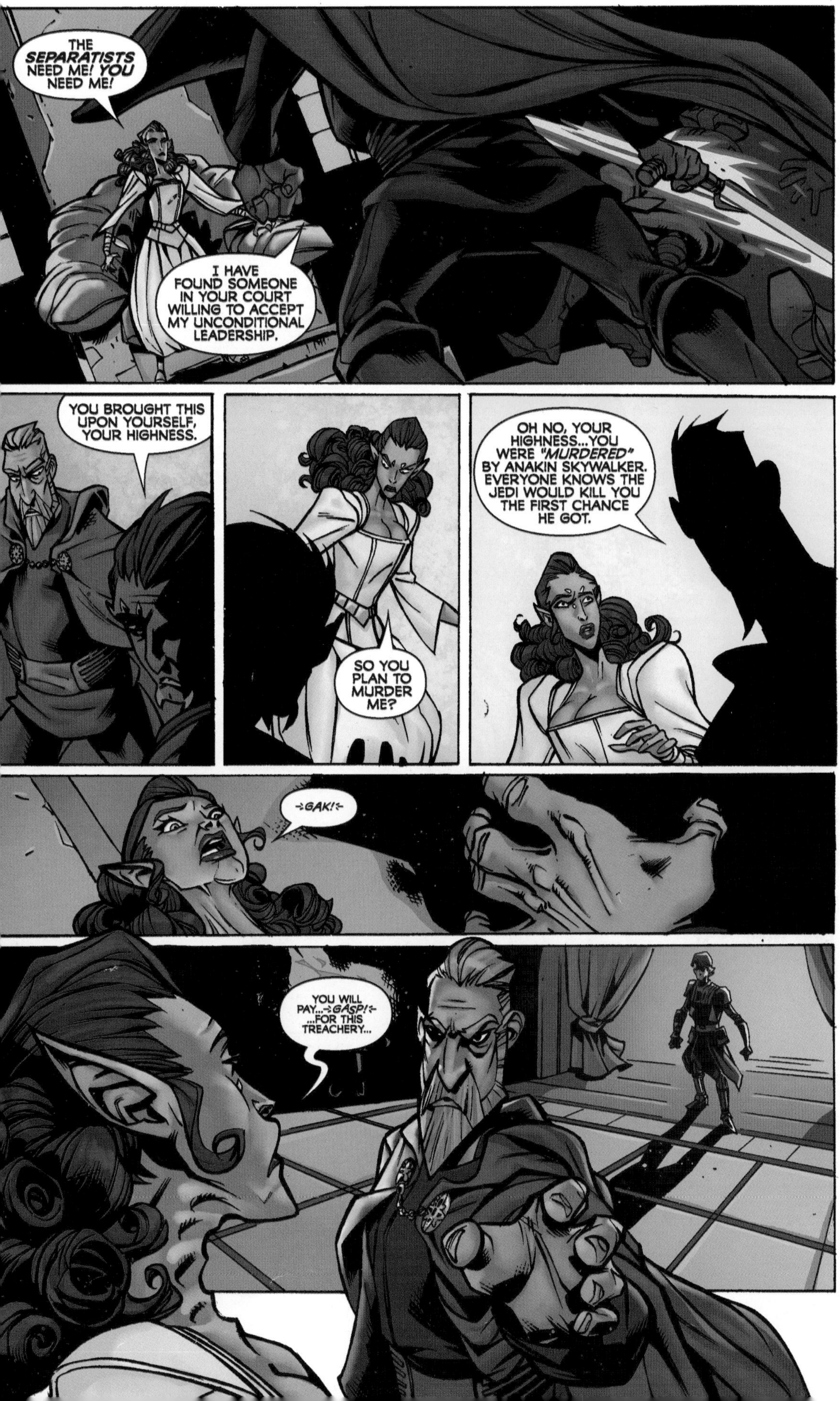
THE SEPARATISTS NEED ME! YOU NEED ME!
I HAVE FOUND SOMEONE IN YOUR COURT WILLING TO ACCEPT MY UNCONDITIONAL LEADERSHIP.
YOU BROUGHT THIS UPON YOURSELF, YOUR HIGHNESS.
SO YOU PLAN TO MURDER ME?
OH NO, YOUR HIGHNESS...YOU WERE "MURDERED" BY ANAKIN SKYWALKER. EVERYONE KNOWS THE JEDI WOULD KILL YOU THE FIRST CHANCE HE GOT.
GAK!
YOU WILL PAY... GASP! ...FOR THIS TREACHERY...

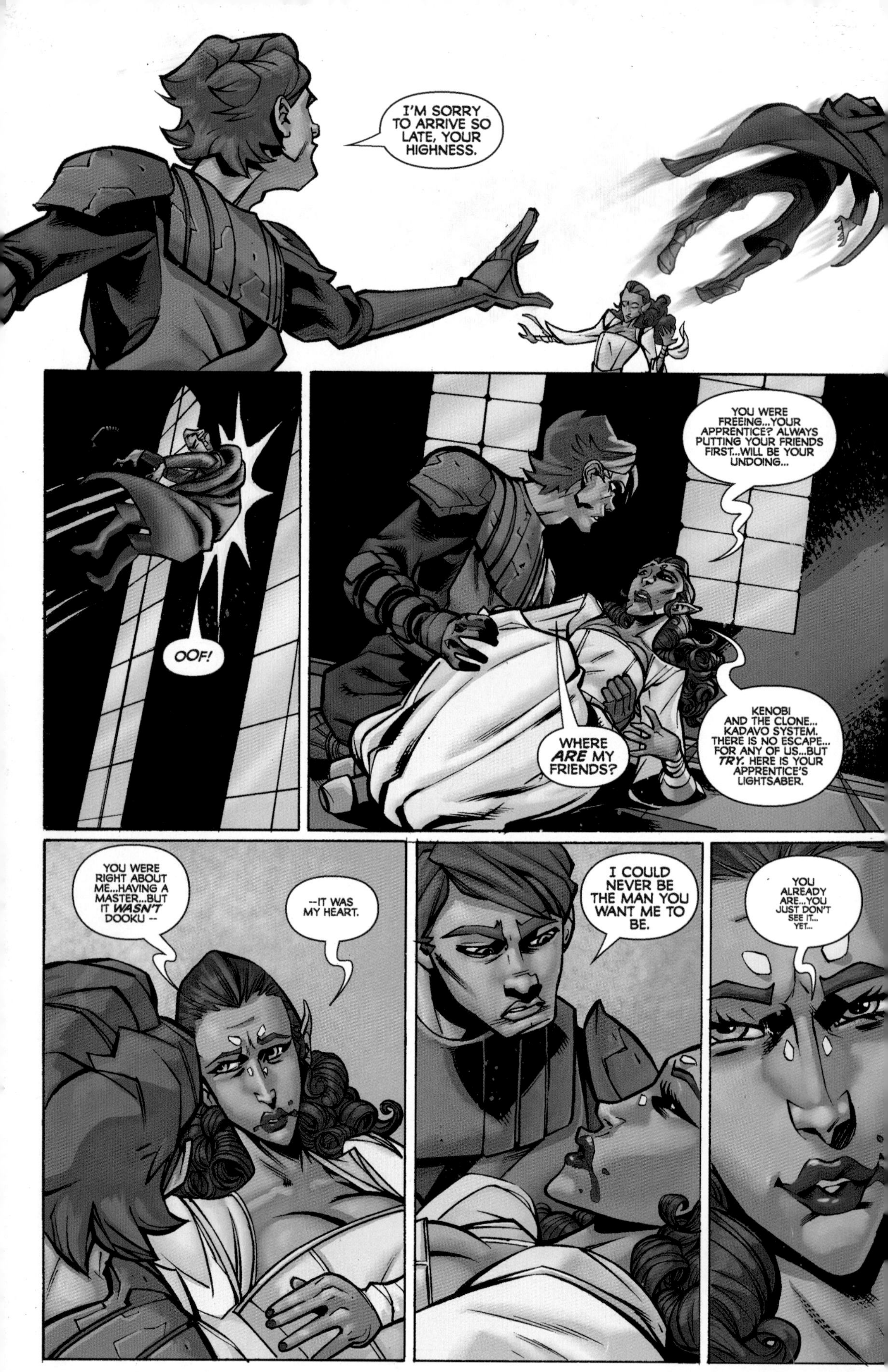
I'M SORRY TO ARRIVE SO LATE, YOUR HIGHNESS.
OOF!
YOU WERE FREEING...YOUR APPRENTICE? ALWAYS PUTTING YOUR FRIENDS FIRST...WILL BE YOUR UNDOING...
WHERE *ARE* MY FRIENDS?
KENOBI AND THE CLONE... KADAVO SYSTEM. THERE IS NO ESCAPE... FOR ANY OF US...BUT *TRY.* HERE IS YOUR APPRENTICE'S LIGHTSABER.
YOU WERE RIGHT ABOUT ME...HAVING A MASTER...BUT IT *WASN'T* DOOKU --
--IT WAS MY HEART.
I COULD NEVER BE THE MAN YOU WANT ME TO BE.
YOU ALREADY ARE...YOU JUST DON'T SEE IT... YET...

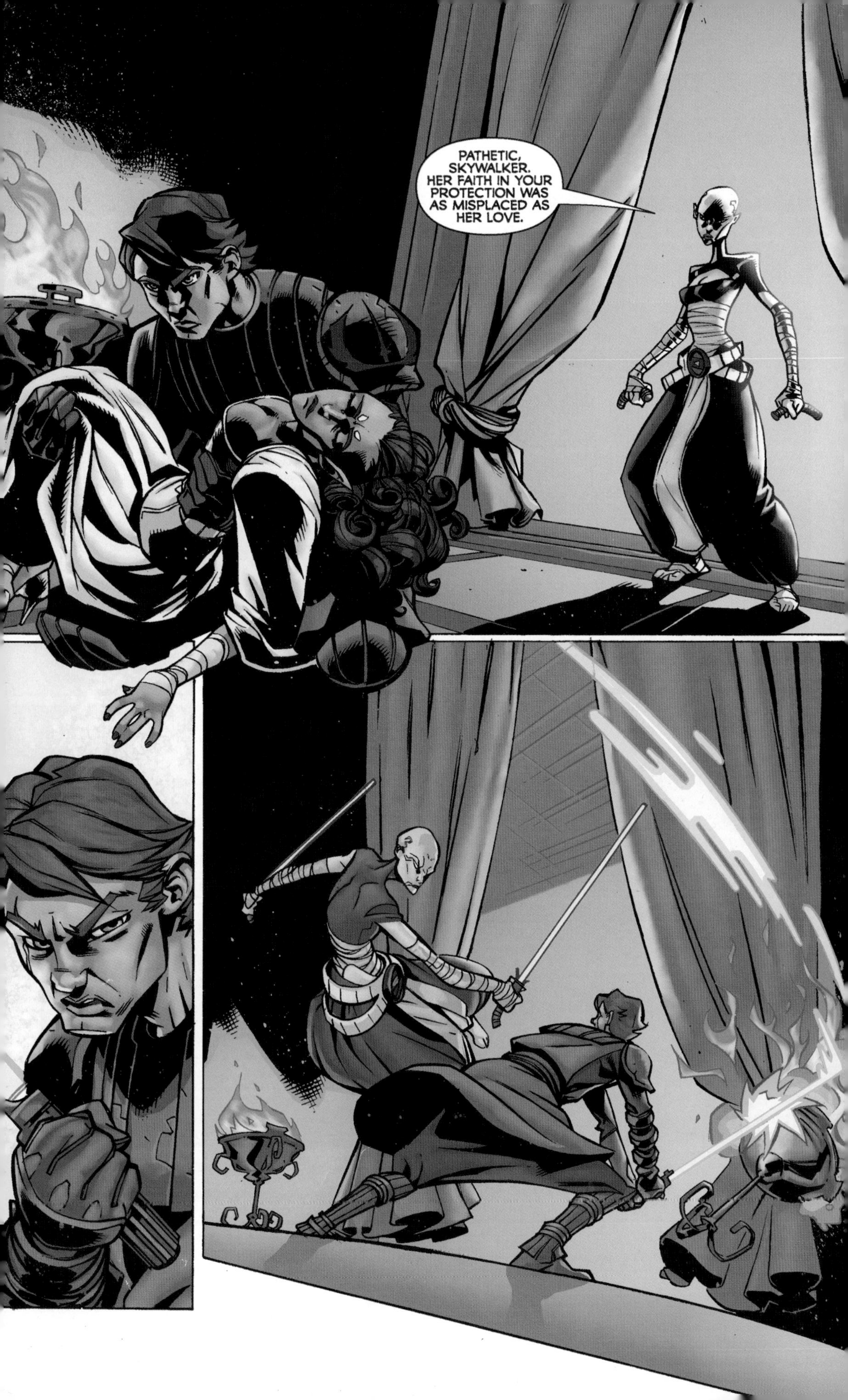
PATHETIC, SKYWALKER. HER FAITH IN YOUR PROTECTION WAS AS MISPLACED AS HER LOVE.

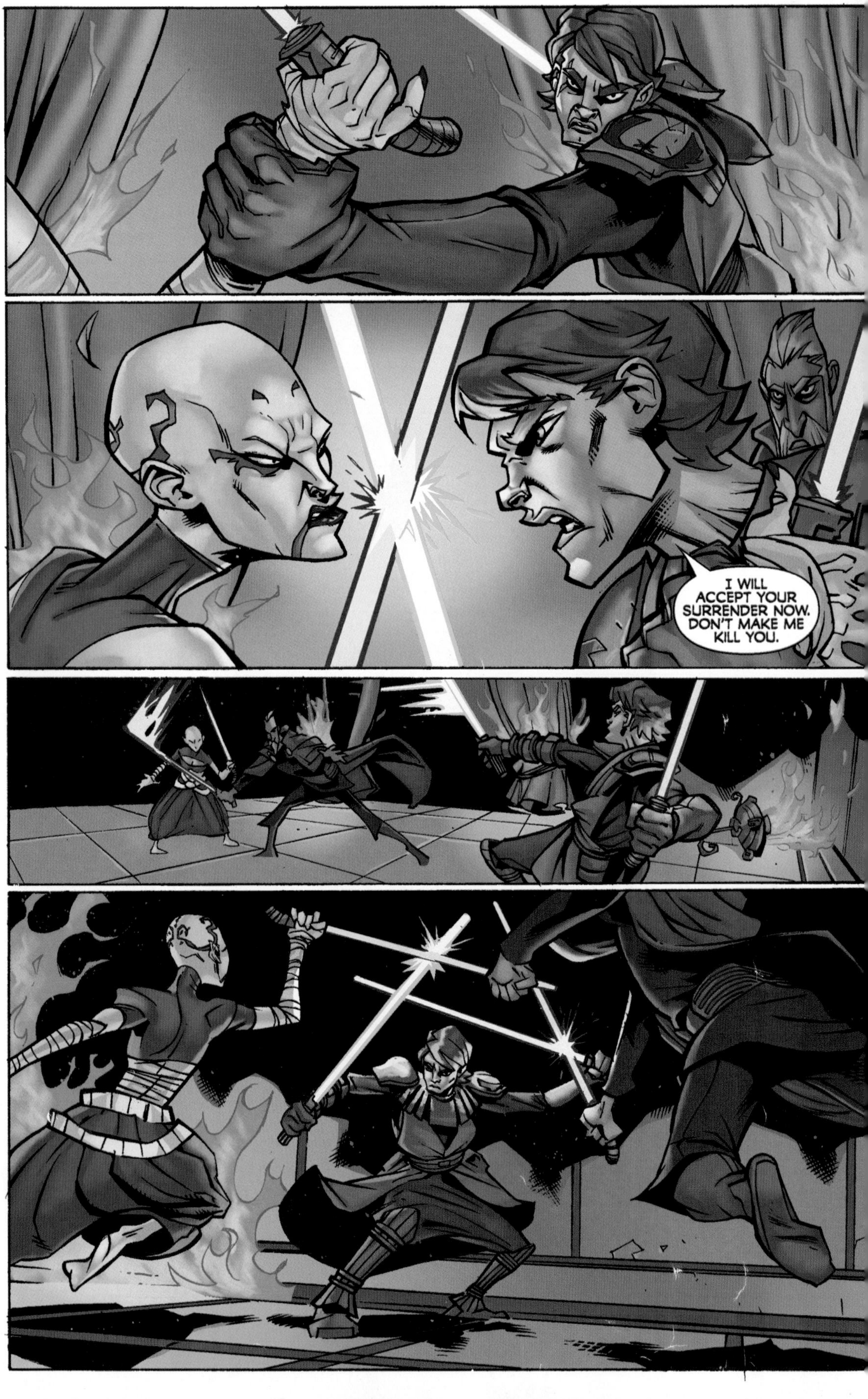
I WILL ACCEPT YOUR SURRENDER NOW. DON'T MAKE ME KILL YOU.

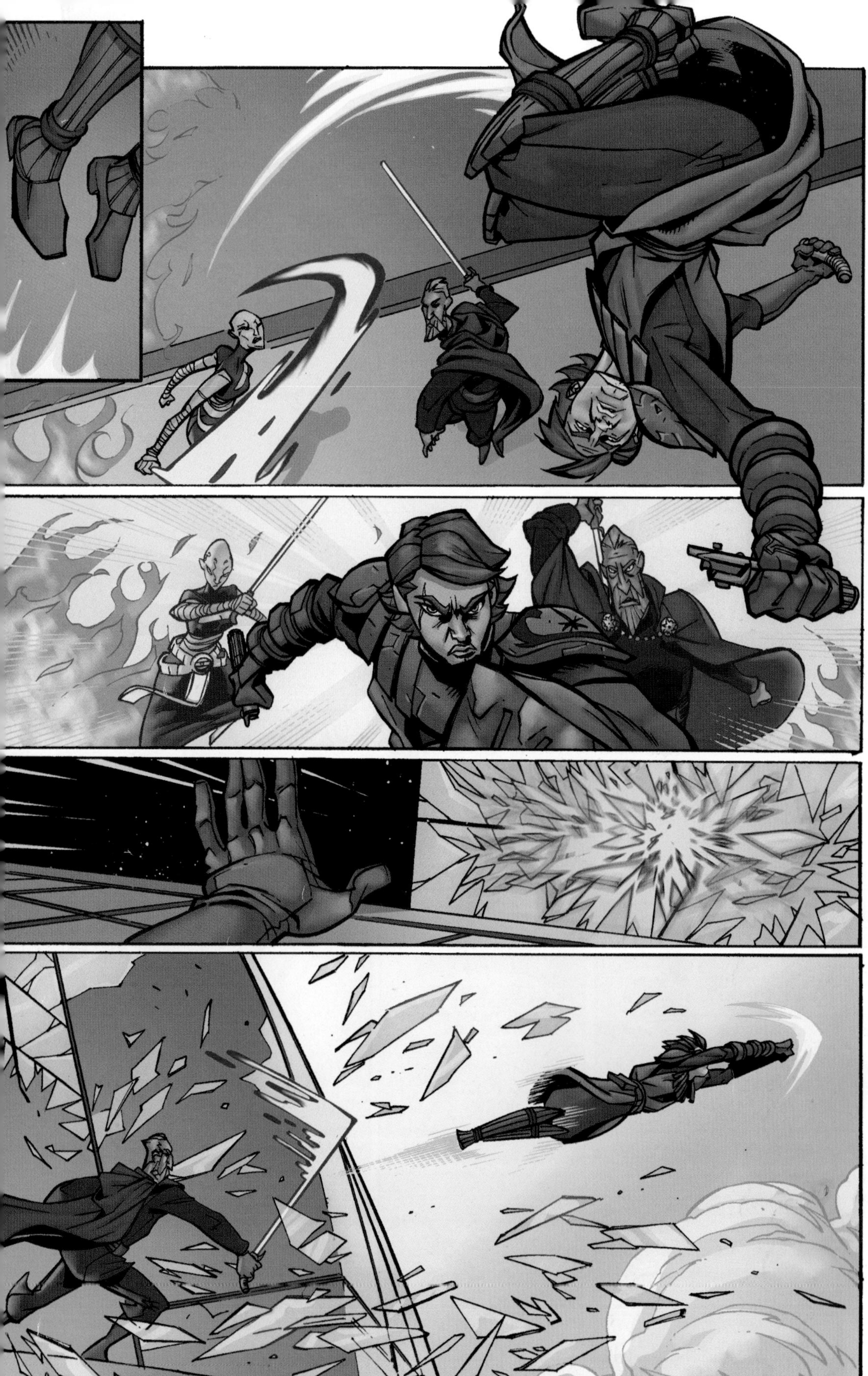

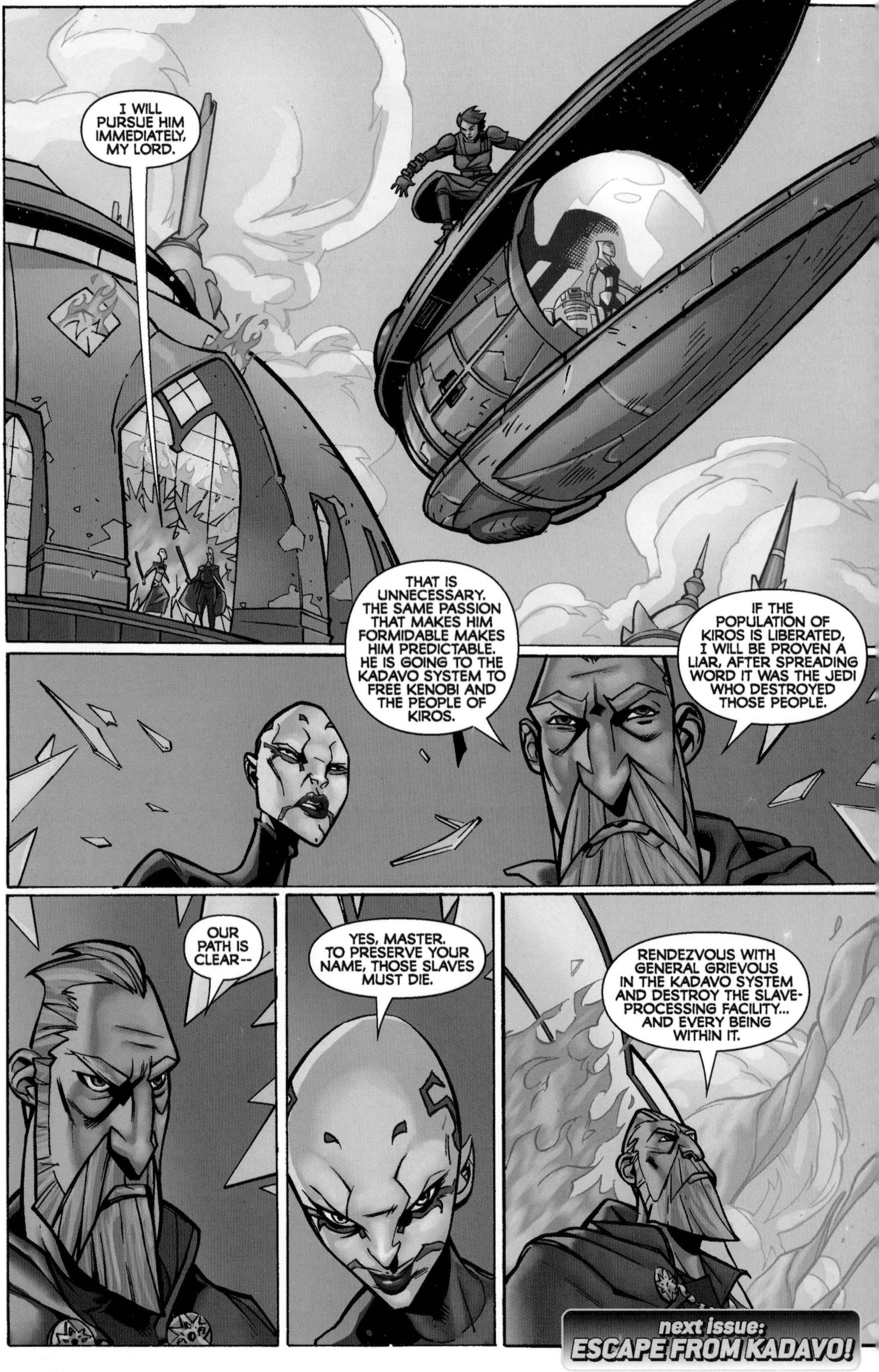
I WILL PURSUE HIM IMMEDIATELY, MY LORD.
THAT IS UNNECESSARY. THE SAME PASSION THAT MAKES HIM FORMIDABLE MAKES HIM PREDICTABLE. HE IS GOING TO THE KADAVO SYSTEM TO FREE KENOBI AND THE PEOPLE OF KIROS.
IF THE POPULATION OF KIROS IS LIBERATED, I WILL BE PROVEN A LIAR, AFTER SPREADING WORD IT WAS THE JEDI WHO DESTROYED THOSE PEOPLE.
OUR PATH IS CLEAR--
YES, MASTER. TO PRESERVE YOUR NAME, THOSE SLAVES MUST DIE.
RENDEZVOUS WITH GENERAL GRIEVOUS IN THE KADAVO SYSTEM AND DESTROY THE SLAVE-PROCESSING FACILITY... AND EVERY BEING WITHIN IT.
next issue:
ESCAPE FROM KADAVO!